For our Michael,
forever remembered
forever loved

www.mascotbooks.com

The Adventures of Kermit the Newf: Dog Tales

Project Newf, LLC
For more information, visit www.KermitTheNewf.com

Illustrations ©2016 Amy Bolin

For more information, please contact:
Mascot Books
560 Herndon Parkway #120
Herndon, VA 20170
info@mascotbooks.com

Library of Congress Control Number: 2015920976

CPSIA Code: PBANG1216B
ISBN: 978-1-63177-591-8

Printed in the United States

THE ADVENTURES OF KERMIT THE NEWF

BOOK 1
DOG TALES

written by
Molly Tischler and Bonnie Giacovelli

illustrated by
Amy Bolin

It was a beautiful sunny day in a little town in Florida. The grass was green and there was a gentle breeze blowing. The trees were blooming beautiful pink flowers.

There were bright yellow and purple flowers on the hedges and tall palm trees everywhere. Some palm trees even had coconuts hanging from them.

Kermit the big, black and white Newfoundland dog came out of his house with his owner, Miss Bonnie. He sniffed the grass and hedges and thought, *What a wonderful day this is. It's the perfect day for an outing!*

"Grandma's coming to pick us up!" Miss Bonnie said excitedly.

Great! thought Kermit. *I love riding in her big minivan!*

He never knew where they were going when Grandma picked them up, but wherever they went, it was always fun. Sometimes they went to the park, where he could run around without a leash.

Sometimes they went to the beach where he could play in the big blue ocean.

Other times they just walked around downtown, where people would stop to pet him and ask his name.

Kermit loved going to all of these places.

When Grandma arrived she opened the back door, and Kermit rushed in and gave her a lick on her face and got her all wet.

"Hi, Kermit!" Grandma said, wiping her face with a towel. She was always prepared for Kermit's licks. "You need your face wiped, too. Are you ready to go to the LIBRARY?"

The library is my favorite place in the whole world! thought Kermit.

On the ride to the library, Kermit laid down on the back seat and took a nap. But as soon as they got off the highway, he sat up and looked out the window. When he sat up, he was bigger than both Miss Bonnie and Grandma.

"He knows where we're going," said Grandma laughing.
"Almost there, Kermit!"

Kermit got so excited he couldn't stop wagging his big, black and white tail. It doesn't just wag from side to side, like other dogs' tails, it wags in crazy directions.

Up and down, figure eights, and around in circles. Round and round, first one way then the other.

"His tail looks like it's going to fly off just like a helicopter!" Miss Bonnie said.

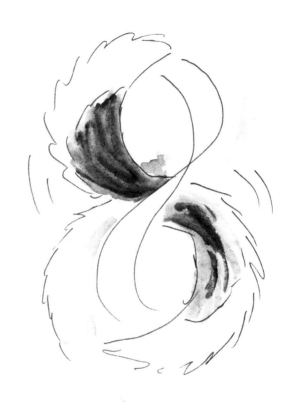

In the library, Miss Bonnie and Grandma said hello to the guard and the librarians. Kermit, of course, greeted them by wagging his crazy tail. Then they rode the elevator up to the third floor.

As soon as the elevator doors opened, Kermit headed straight for the children's section.

Read to me and I will dream... Of man

Kermit had his own area in the children's section. *This is my favorite spot,* Kermit thought as he laid down in his bean bag chair. Children were already waiting to read books to Kermit.

Miss Bonnie joined Kermit on the bean bag chair. Soon, children were coming over with books to read to Kermit. He liked listening to the stories and being petted by the children while they read.

A little boy named Michael came into the children's section. He had been coming to the library for many weeks, but he was very shy and never went near Kermit. Each week he would look at Kermit, from behind his mother's legs, then he would run to the back of the library. NO DOGS FOR HIM.

Every week, Kermit watched him run away. *I wonder why that nice little boy won't read to me and pet me,* Kermit thought. But Kermit also noticed every week Michael would sneak back to where he was and watch the other children read to him.

Michael watched as a little boy read to Kermit and then gave him a cookie. Miss Bonnie gave the little boy his own book to take home and keep.

Next, he watched a girl
read to Kermit and give
him a cookie and she got
a book to take home too.
Each week he watched and
each week, Kermit noticed
he came a little closer.

Michael was very curious about this big, black and white dog who just laid there and let the children pet him and read to him.

That dog isn't biting them or even barking at them, Michael thought. *Maybe I could try reading to him too.*

Kermit saw Michael watching him. He knew if he just laid down on the floor and waited patiently while he enjoyed hearing the stories, and of course eating cookies, there was a chance Michael would read to him too.

So Kermit laid very still, looked at Michael, and wagged just the very tip of his tail.

Quietly and cautiously, Michael came over to Miss Bonnie and said, "Can I read to him, please?"

"Of course you can," Miss Bonnie replied. "Just pick a book from the red bucket and you'll be next."

Michael picked a short book to read. He didn't want to stay too long.

Michael's hands shook as he held the book and started to read. Miss Bonnie helped him with the big words and they looked at the pictures together. He didn't pet Kermit or give him a cookie, but that was okay. He had the courage to read to the big dog.

Every week after that Michael went to the library ready to read to Kermit. He even laid down on the floor and put his head on Kermit's furry belly!

He fed Kermit cookies, petted his furry coat, and rubbed his face in Kermit's hair. It tickled his nose and made him laugh. The best thing of all was when Kermit licked his face.

"I like big, black and white fluffy dogs now," Michael told Kermit one day. "I'm not afraid anymore." Then he gave Kermit a big hug and Kermit gave him a big lick on his cheek, which made Michael laugh again.

Now Kermit and Michael are best pals. They look forward to being together at the library every week.

And every week Kermit thinks, *I'm so happy that Michael's not afraid of me anymore. I'm so gentle, I'd never hurt anyone. I'm just like a big teddy bear, ready for lots of love and hugs.*

Left to Right: Bonnie Giacovelli, Kermit the Newf, Molly Tischler

Molly Tischler is Bonnie's mother. Upon retiring from a career as a Financial Advisor, she decided to pursue her lifelong passion for writing. What better subject could there be than her real life adventures with Kermit the Newf. She lives in Juno Beach, Florida with her husband, Stephen.

Bonnie Giacovelli is a graduate of The College of the Atlantic, where she earned a Bachelor's Degree in Human Ecology with a major in Zoology. She was diagnosed with Multiple Sclerosis more than twenty years ago. She is visually impaired and has balance issues. She trains her own service dogs to accommodate her needs. Kermit is her third service dog. She lives in Jupiter, Florida, with her husband, Lenny and her other dogs and cats.

Kermit is an 8 ½-year-old Newfoundland dog, born and raised in Florida. He is a service dog, therapy dog, draft dog, model, and actor. He has been nominated three years in row for the AKC Humane Fund's ACE award, Achievement in Canine Excellence, in the therapy dog category. In 2013, he won Honorable Mention. He has done TV commercials, print ads, and corporate meet and greets. He has been in show business since he was eleven months old and has more than two dozen jobs to his credit. He enjoys competing in obedience, rally obedience, and conformation showing. He is also training to do water rescue. He is kind, gentle, sweet, and very intelligent. He loves people, especially children. His registered name is Rockbottom's Color Me Bad at Shagganappi, RN, DD5, CD, THDX, CI, CGC. (RN=rally obedience novice title; DD5= draft dog title with 5 re-qualifications; CD= companion dog obedience title; THDX= therapy dog excellent title; CI= carting intermediate title; CGC= canine good citizen title)

Amy Bolin is living her childhood dream of drawing, painting, and sculpting dogs for a living. *Dog Tales* is the first book she has illustrated, and she looks forward to illustrating many more! She lives in northern Michigan with her husband Troy, three sons Jesse, Nile, and Gene, an orange cat named Cheese, and a Saint Bernard named Sadie.